MW00634342

THE POLICEMAN AND THE DOG WHO ALWAYS CAUGHT THE BAD GUYS

By Miles M. Pines

Illustrated by Taillefer Long

Copyright © 2011 by Pines Publishers LLC All rights reserved.

Pines Publishers LLC
PO Box 170627
Austin, TX 78717
www.PinesPublishers.com

LCCN: 2011922878

ISBN: 978-0-9833708-0-2 (paperback)
        978-0-9833708-1-9 (hardback)

To my family and the color yellow.

There once was a policeman and a dog who loved each other. They lived in a town called Pumpkinville, and they were very happy together. The policeman's name was Officer Cherries, and the dog's name was Hunter.

They loved working with each other very much, and they always caught the bad guys—no matter how long it took them. The bad guys never got away in Pumpkinville!

Every time Officer Cherries and Hunter sent a bad guy to jail, Officer Cherries baked pies so that everyone in town could celebrate. People came from all over the county to eat the special celebration pies.

The pies were the best pies in the world. They were made from fresh pumpkins that grew on the farms of Pumpkinville. Officer Cherries served the pies with a special mixed juice drink he called a "juice concoction."

After celebrating, everyone would go home full but very happy. They were so glad to be safe and sound and well fed too!

One day in Pumpkinville there was a twister—a huge tornado that destroyed the whole town. It was a disaster.

The walls of the jail crumbled to the ground.
All five of the criminals in Pumpkinville escaped.

The day after the twister, the good citizens of Pumpkinville gathered around in the town square. Together they came up with a plan to rebuild the town. First they would rebuild their homes. Then they would rebuild the hospital, and then the library, the stores, and the police station. And finally, they would build a new jail for bad guys.

But what were they going to do about the five criminals who escaped? Officer Cherries told the citizens not to worry. He said that he and Hunter (maybe with a little help from some friends) would track down each and every bad guy and keep everyone safe, no matter what.

"We are on it, and we have it covered," Officer Cherries reassured the crowd. "You all focus on rebuilding your town. Hunter and I will take care of the bad guys."

So Officer Cherries and Hunter ran off to recruit more policemen because it was only the two of them.

CHERRIES
NTER

OFFICER
MANGO

OFFICER
LEMON

They found four other policemen (retired officers Grapefruit, Kiwi, Mango and Lemon) who were willing to join in the hunt for the bad guys.

Officer Cherries briefed the others about the five bad guys. "This is what we are up against," said Officer Cherries. "All five of the men are very dangerous. The first one is called Ike. He chews on nasty cigars all day long.

"The second is called Maniac. He always eats oranges and throws the peels on the floor.

"The third man is known as Chicken because he only eats chicken. His favorite is fried chicken, but he will pretty much eat any kind of chicken.

WANTED

CHICKEN

IKE

MANIAC

"The fourth bad guy goes by Bananahead because he is always trying to make things out of bananas. He usually just gets frustrated and eats all the bananas.

"And finally, the fifth bad guy is known as Smelly. He never takes a bath or shower and nobody wants to be near him."

When Officer Cherries finished his description, they all set off to find the bad guys.

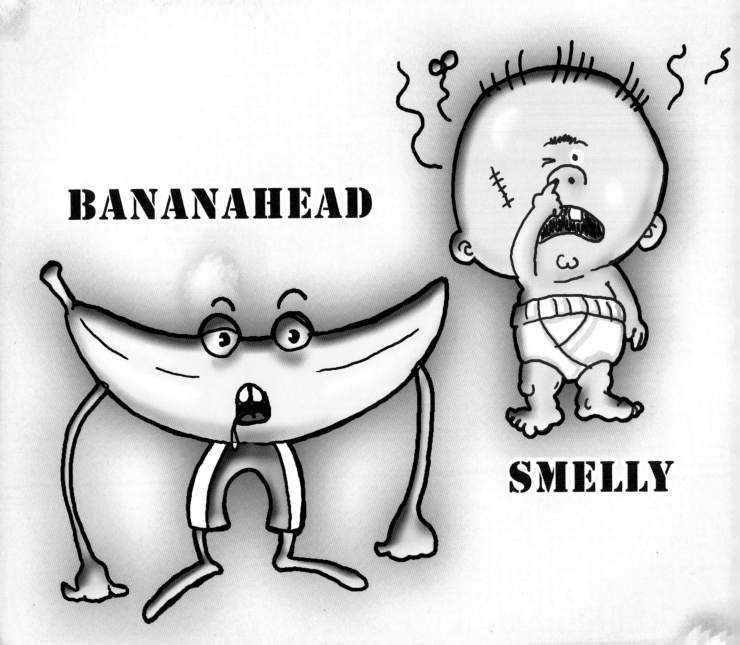

SNIFF
SNIFF

A few weeks went by. The officers carefully searched all the buildings and nearby factories. But there was no trace of the bad guys. Finally, about a month after the big twister, the officers entered an abandoned factory that was in the next county.

Suddenly Hunter's nose twitched and his ears perked up. He smelled something really different in there: the air smelled like stale cigars, orange peels, greasy chicken, ripe bananas, and something that was just plain bad.

Hunter was barking wildly, so Officer Cherries held up his police baton. With his other hand, Officer Cherries shined his flashlight into the corner of the factory. There sitting at a round wooden table were four of the bad guys: Ike, Maniac, Chicken, and Smelly, all playing cards and drinking strong coffee. They were talking loudly and never even noticed Officer Cherries, Hunter, and the others.

Ten feet away stood Bananahead, who was busy trying to make crazy banana weapons of all shapes and sizes for the crew of bad guys. There was a huge pile of banana peels right next to him.

Officer Cherries told the bad guys to freeze. He and Officers Lemon, Mango, and Grapefruit surrounded the bad guys while Officer Kiwi started to handcuff each of them. When Officer Kiwi was finished, the officers took the bad guys back to Pumpkinville and put them in the brand-new Pumpkinville jail.

Everyone in town was relieved and knew what was going to come next: a special celebration with the world's best pies!

The pies were more scrumptious than ever. And the juice concoction was the tastiest, fruitiest, and most thirst-quenching drink that anyone in Pumpkinville had ever tasted.

After the party, everyone went home full and happy. But nobody was as happy as Officer Cherries and his wonderful police dog, Hunter.

They felt great because they knew that they had once again **saved the day.** After that, all of the citizens of Pumpkinville lived **happily** and **safely** ever after.

18359582R00015

Made in the USA
Lexington, KY
30 October 2012